The Smallest Gift of CHRISTMAS

PETER H. REYNOLDS

WALKER BOOKS
AND SUBSIDIARIES
LONDON · BOSTON · SYDNEY · AUCKLAND

Roland was eager for Christmas Day.

He raced downstairs to see what
was waiting for him.

But when he saw his present,
he was not impressed.
It was the smallest gift
he had _ever_ seen.

Had he waited the whole year
for this tiny gift?

Roland closed his eyes and hoped and wished as hard as he could for a BIGGER gift.

And when he opened his eyes,
there WAS a bigger gift!

"You call THAT big?" Roland asked.
He had been wishing for something
MUCH bigger. He closed his eyes
and wished a bit harder.

"Ha! That one isn't much bigger than me,"
Roland said. "And <u>I'm</u> not very big!"

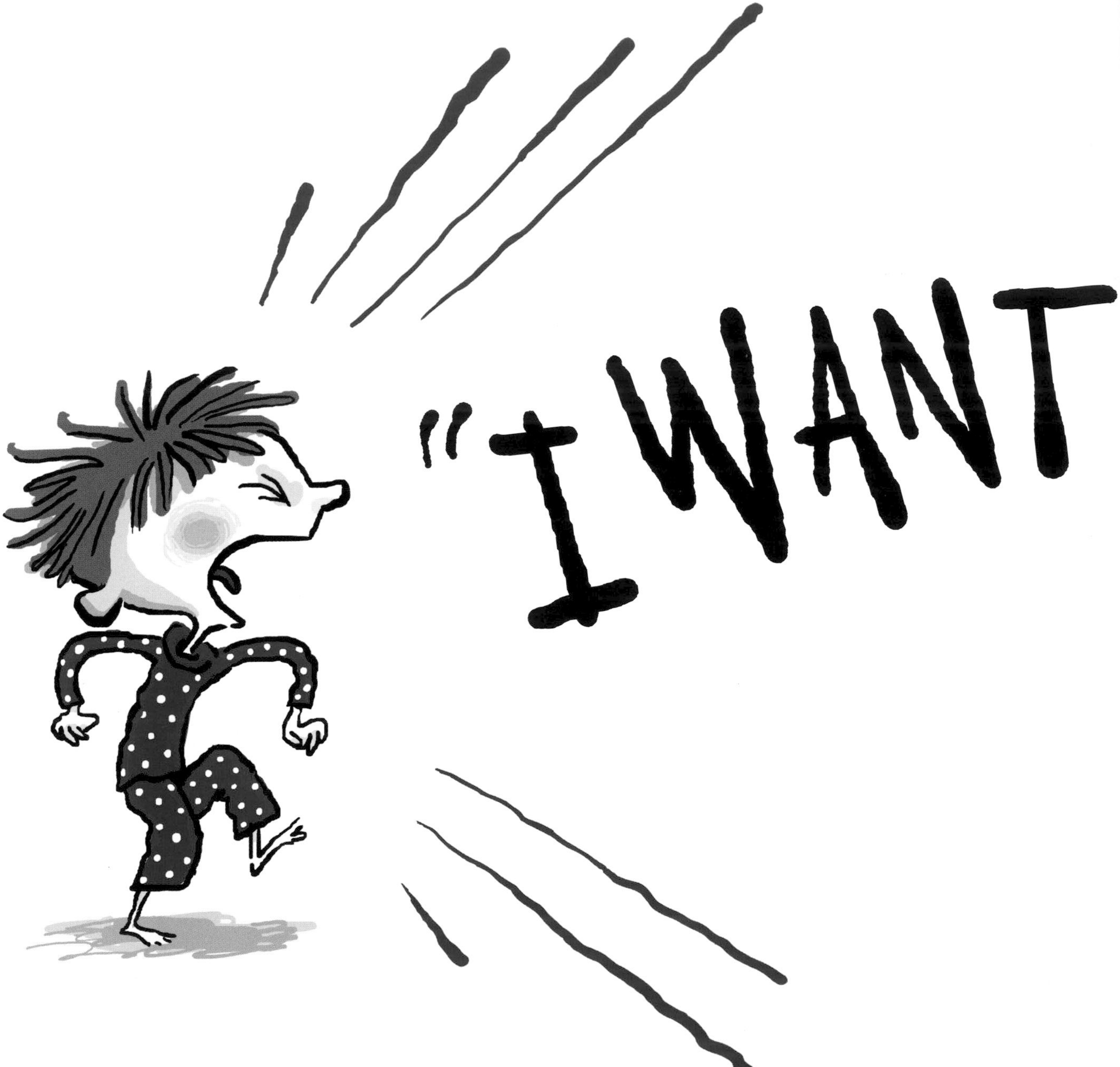
"I WANT

A BIGGER

GIFT!"

"BIG? That's not even as big as my house! When I say big, I mean BIG!" he yelled.

Roland stomped off, sure there was a bigger gift for him—<u>somewhere</u>.

In the distance, he saw a present
wedged between two buildings.

Now <u>THAT</u>, Roland thought, <u>that</u>
is pretty big. But still not big enough!

Roland was determined.

So he set off to search the universe.

He searched and searched, but all he could see were billions of stars.

Roland peered into his telescope.

He could just make out a
tiny dot in the distance.

Earth! His home, his family...
now just a speck, growing
smaller and smaller.

Roland realized that he was very,
VERY far from home and that
if he waited a heartbeat longer,
that little dot would disappear.

Roland had never thought he'd want
something so small so badly.

He closed his eyes and hoped and wished with all his might for that tiny speck—the smallest gift.

As the rocket headed towards it,
the dot grew **bigger** and **bigger.**

As Roland's rocket landed gently,

he realized that the smallest speck
<u>was</u> his biggest gift.

Roland was home.

Merry Christmas!

To Henry Rocket Reynolds

First published 2013 by Walker Books Ltd
87 Vauxhall Walk, London SE11 5HJ

2 4 6 8 10 9 7 5 3 1

© 2013 Peter H. Reynolds

The right of Peter H. Reynolds to be identified as author/illustrator of this work
has been asserted by him in accordance with the Copyright, Designs and Patents Act 1988

This book has been hand-lettered by Peter H. Reynolds

Printed in China

British Library Cataloguing in Publication Data:
a catalogue record for this book is available from the British Library

ISBN 978-1-4063-4991-7

www.walker.co.uk